Dear Parent:
Your child's love of reading starts here!

Every child learns to read in a different way and at his or her own speed. Some go back and forth between reading levels and read favorite books again and again. Others read through each level in order. You can help your young reader improve and become more confident by encouraging his or her own interests and abilities. From books your child reads with you to the first books he or she reads alone, there are I Can Read Books for every stage of reading:

SHARED READING
Basic language, word repetition, and whimsical illustrations, ideal for sharing with your emergent reader

BEGINNING READING
Short sentences, familiar words, and simple concepts for children eager to read on their own

READING WITH HELP
Engaging stories, longer sentences, and language play for developing readers

READING ALONE
Complex plots, challenging vocabulary, and high-interest topics for the independent reader

ADVANCED READING
Short paragraphs, chapters, and exciting themes for the perfect bridge to chapter books

I Can Read Books have introduced children to the joy of reading since 1957. Featuring award-winning authors and illustrators and a fabulous cast of beloved characters, I Can Read Books set the standard for beginning readers.

A lifetime of discovery begins with the magical words **"I Can Read!"**

Visit www.icanread.com for information
on enriching your child's reading experience.

I Can Read Book® is a trademark of HarperCollins Publishers.

Dixie and the Good Deeds
Copyright © 2013 by HarperCollins Publishers. All rights reserved. Printed in the United States of America. No part of this book may be used or reproduced in any manner whatsoever without written permission except in the case of brief quotations embodied in critical articles and reviews. For information address HarperCollins Children's Books, a division of HarperCollins Publishers, 10 East 53rd Street, New York, NY 10022.
www.icanread.com
Library of Congress catalog card number: 2012953624
ISBN 978-0-06-208657-0 (trade bdg.) –ISBN 978-0-06-208643-3 (pbk.)

13 14 15 16 17   LP/WOR   10 9 8 7 6 5 4 3 2 1   ❖   First Edition

I Can Read!

BEGINNING 1 READING

Dixie

and the
Good Deeds

story by Grace Gilman

pictures by Sarah McConnell

HARPER

An Imprint of HarperCollinsPublishers

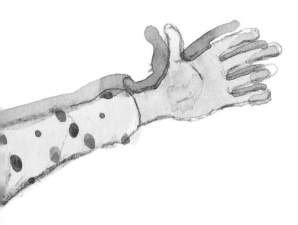

"I have a new school project,"

Emma said to Dixie.

"I have to volunteer around town."

Dixie wagged her tail.

She wanted to help.

"My teacher told us lots of ways
we could be helpful," said Emma.
"I signed up for all of them!"
Emma hadn't realized that she
had to do everything on Saturday.

On Saturday, Dixie made sure
Emma woke up early.

While the sun rose, Emma baked cookies
for the library bake sale.
The money would be used
to buy more books for the library.

While the cookies were baking,

Emma started to clean up.

Dixie wanted to help.

Dixie reached for the flour.

"No, Dixie!" said Emma.

It was too late.

Flour spilled everywhere!

"Oh, Dixie," said Emma.

"I have no time to give you a bath.

We have to go!"

Emma got to the bake sale
just in time.
But she couldn't stay long.
This was only her first good deed
of the day.

It was Recycling Day at the park.

Emma collected bottles and cans.

Dixie wanted to recycle too.

She reached for a bottle.

"That's my juice!" said a boy.

But it was too late.

The juice spilled all over Dixie,

making her sticky.

"Sorry," Emma said to the boy.

Then she left for Town Square.

Emma helped paint the new fence.

Dixie wanted to help.

"Not this time," said Emma.

"You might spill the paint."

Dixie did not spill the paint.

She stepped in it!

What a mess!

But Emma had no time to clean up.

She had to rush off to the car wash.

The car wash was going to raise money

for a rock wall in the school gym.

Emma scrubbed car after car.

Dixie wanted to help with the hose.

"No, Dixie!" said Emma.

Emma was too late.

Dixie was soaked!

"Come on, Dixie!" said Emma.

"We have to go to the town garden."

Emma was the only helper
to show up at the garden.
"I don't have time to plant
everything myself,"
Emma told Dixie.

Dixie wanted to help.

"Well…okay," said Emma.

"But please be careful!"

Dixie got to work, digging holes

as quickly as she could.

Emma followed along,

planting flowers.

She couldn't have done it without Dixie!

On her way to Hobble Hall

for her magic show,

Emma dropped off Dixie at home.

"I can't bring you this time," said Emma.

Dixie looked sad.

She wanted to go with Emma.

When Emma got to Hobble Hall,

the seats were already filled.

She hardly had any time

to set up her magic tricks.

"Meet Emma the magician!"
said a man.

Everyone clapped.

Emma felt nervous.

Emma reached into her pocket.
"I'm going to make a dime
disappear," she said.
But Emma had forgotten her
trick coins at home.

"Pick a card," Emma said to a man.
"Then put it back in the deck
and I'll tell you what it was."
The man did as Emma asked.
Emma looked through the deck.

"Aha!" said Emma.

"Your card was the three of spades."

"Wrong," said the man.

"My card was the six of spades."

"Oops," said Emma.

Things were not going well!

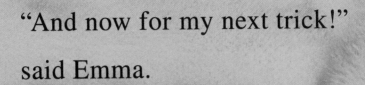

"And now for my next trick!"
said Emma.
"I'm going to pull a rabbit
out of a hat."

Oh, no! thought Emma.

There was no rabbit!

Emma didn't know what to do,

so she said the magic word:

"Abracadabra."

As if by magic, the rabbit appeared.

It was not in the hat.

Dixie had it!

Everyone clapped—including Emma.

Dixie had saved the show.

Emma hugged Dixie.

"Thanks for finding the rabbit
and following me," she said.

Dixie licked Emma's face.

They were both tired.

It had been a long day.

On Monday, Emma told her class about her good deeds.

"I didn't do it alone," she said. "My dog, Dixie, did a great deed by helping me."